Miley the Stylist Fairy

Special thanks to Narinder Dhami

ISBN 978-0-545-48478-7

Previously published as *Pop Star Fairies #4: Miley the Stylist Fairy* by Orchard U.K. in 2012.

All rights reserved. Published by Scholastic Inc., 557 Broadway, New York, NY 10012, by arrangement with Rainbow Magic Limited.

12 11 10 9 8 7 6 5 4 3 2 1   13 14 15 16 17 18/0

Printed in the U.S.A.   40

This edition first printing, March 2013

Miley the Stylist Fairy

by Daisy Meadows

SCHOLASTIC INC.

Jack Frost's Ice Castle

Campsite

Girls' tent

Main Stage

Karaoke tent

Café

The Harbor

Rainspell

Island

It's about time for the world to see
The legend I was born to be.
The prince of pop, a dazzling star,
My fans will flock from near and far.

But superstar fame is hard to get
Unless I help myself, I bet.
I need a plan, a cunning trick
To make my stage act super-slick.

Seven magic clefs I'll steal —
They'll give me true superstar appeal.
I'll sing and dance, I'll dazzle and shine,
And superstar glory will be mine!

Contents

Clashing Clothes

"What's that noise?" Rachel murmured sleepily. She could hear a steady *pitter-patter* sound on the roof of the tent above her. Yawning, Rachel sat up in her sleeping bag. At the same time, her best friend, Kirsty, stirred and opened her eyes.

"Oh, it's *raining!*" Rachel exclaimed, suddenly realizing what the noise was.

Kirsty sat up, too. "Is that thunder?" she asked a little nervously as a loud rumble echoed through the tent.

Rachel laughed. "No, that's my dad snoring in the other section of the tent!" she explained. Scrambling out of her sleeping bag, she went over to the tent's main entrance. Kirsty followed, and together the two girls looked out.

The site of the Rainspell Island Music Festival was soggy with heavy rain. It was morning, but the sky was dark and threatening. The grassy fields where the tents, stages, and performers' trailers had been set up were already turning to mud.

"What a shame!" Kirsty remarked. "Especially since we had such amazing weather yesterday."

"It doesn't matter whether it's sunny or rainy, though, does it?" Rachel reminded her. "We still have to keep looking for the Superstar Fairies' magic clefs!"

Kirsty nodded. "I wonder which fairy we'll help today," she said.

When the girls had arrived on Rainspell Island the day before, they'd discovered that Jack Frost and his goblins had stolen the Superstar Fairies' clefs, the magical items that helped them ensure that superstars everywhere gave great performances.

It was Jack Frost's dream to be the richest and most famous superstar in the whole world, and he planned to use the power of the clefs to perform at the Rainspell Festival. Rachel and Kirsty had promised to help the fairies get the magic clefs back, because without them, pop music in both the human and the fairy worlds would be ruined for everyone. So far, the girls, along with Jessie the Lyrics Fairy, Adele the Voice Fairy, and Vanessa the Choreography Fairy, had rescued three of the clefs from the goblins who were hiding them.

"We saw three fantastic concerts yesterday, didn't we?" Rachel remarked as she and Kirsty went back to their sleeping area. "It's good that Jessie, Adele, and Vanessa got their clefs back in time,

and that they had *just* enough magic to help The Angels, A-OK, and Sasha Sharp perform well."

"But the Superstar Fairies need *all* the magic clefs for things to be right again." Kirsty sighed. "And even though we've seen the goblins, we still haven't found Jack Frost! I wish we knew where he was hiding."

Rachel glanced at her watch. "We'd better get dressed," she said. "We're supposed to meet The Angels for a pancake brunch at the Harbor Café, remember?"

The girls had become friends with the famous singing group The Angels after winning a competition to meet them. Lexy, Emilia, and Serena had even invited Rachel and Kirsty to the Rainspell Island Music Festival as their special guests.

Kirsty and Rachel went over to the corner of their sleeping area where they'd put the duffel bags full of their clothes. Suddenly, Kirsty gasped as a raindrop hit her nose.

"Where did *that* come from?" Kirsty asked, glancing upward. To her dismay, she saw a small  rip in the tent roof. Rain was leaking in and falling on the bags directly underneath.

"Our bags are soaked!" Rachel groaned.

"And that means our clothes are probably soaked, too." Kirsty sighed. She opened her bag and pulled out a couple of wet T-shirts. "Yes, they are!"

"We must have *something* dry enough to wear." Rachel began digging urgently through the damp contents of her bag. "We can't meet up with The Angels in our pajamas!"

The girls searched through their clothes.

"The things at the bottom of my bag are still dry," Kirsty said. She pulled out a long pink skirt printed with yellow flowers and a green T-shirt with white polka dots. "I'll have to wear these, but they don't exactly go together!"

"Mine either!" Rachel said with a grin, holding up a pair of purple and white striped leggings and a red plaid shirt. "But they're all I have."

Quickly, the girls dressed in their mismatched outfits. They looked at each other and burst out laughing.

"Oh, well, I guess rain and mud and funny clothes are all part of being at a music festival," Kirsty said. "I think we should take a picture of ourselves!" She grabbed her camera and, holding it out

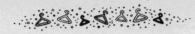

in front of
her, took
a picture of
Rachel and
herself.

"At least
we have
raincoats,
umbrellas, and
rain boots, too,"
said Rachel.

The girls put on
their raincoats, and
both of them slipped their cameras into
their pockets. Then, pulling on their
boots, they headed out. On the way,
they called to Rachel's parents in the
other sleeping area and warned them
about the leak.

"Your dad and I will figure it out while you're gone," Mrs. Walker promised. "We'll see you at the concert later."

Rachel and Kirsty stepped out of the tent into the pouring rain.

"I hope it stops raining for the concert this afternoon," Rachel remarked, struggling to put her umbrella up against the strong wind.

Kirsty opened her umbrella, too. Immediately, a shower of rainbow-colored glitter tumbled out, followed by a tiny fairy.

"It's Miley the Stylist Fairy!" Kirsty exclaimed.

At the Harbor Café

Miley smiled at the girls, shaking the dazzling fairy dust from her long brown hair. She wore a denim mini skirt with leggings and a blue hoodie. Orange sneakers sparkled on her feet.

"Isn't this weather awful, girls?" Miley cried, hovering under the shelter of Kirsty's umbrella. "Of course, you know

why I'm here — to find my magic clef. Without it, all the superstars' special, stylish clothes will be ruined!"

"Yes, it will be terrible if the superstars have to wear silly outfits like the ones Kirsty and I have on!" Rachel agreed. "We're just on our way to meet The Angels at the Harbor Café, Miley."

"We can keep an eye out for your clef on the way," Kirsty added.

"Wonderful!" Miley smiled at them. "I'll stay out of sight up here." She fluttered up to the top of Kirsty's umbrella and perched on one of the spokes.

The girls began to make their way across the festival site. Even though it was raining heavily, people were still out and about in rubber boots and raincoats.

"Star Village is just as busy as usual, even though it's raining," Rachel remarked as they trudged through the mud. Star Village was a group of tents where people could try out different superstar activities like dressing up, singing karaoke, and learning dance routines.

Suddenly, Kirsty grabbed Rachel's arm. "Stay away from those boys over there, Rachel," she murmured. "They're splashing everyone with mud!"

Rachel glanced around and saw a gang of boys wearing long, bright green raincoats, large rain hats pulled down over their faces, and huge boots. The boys were pretending to perform a dance routine, but Rachel could see that they were just jumping around in the puddles and splattering everyone who went past with muddy water.

"Thanks, Kirsty," Rachel said as they walked by, keeping far away from the mischievous boys. "Someone's going to get really upset with them in a minute!"

The girls continued through the festival site, keeping a lookout for the magic music clef. But there was no sign of it, and they didn't see any goblins, either. They left the site and headed for the Harbor Café, which was located in Rainspell's pretty little harbor overlooking the sandy beach.

When they reached the café, the girls stopped under the red-and-white-striped awning to close their umbrellas. Miley zoomed out and neatly hid herself inside the pocket of Rachel's plaid shirt.

"Look, Rachel." Kirsty pointed with the tip of her umbrella at a colorful poster stuck in the café window. "It's The Groove Gang! I can't wait to see their concert this afternoon."

"They look so cool," Rachel said, studying the poster. The five members of The Groove Gang each wore a special color — Yvette's hoodie and sneakers were yellow, Rick wore red, Blake blue, Lila lilac, and Paige was pretty in pink. The same five colors had been used in swirling patterns all over the background of the poster.

"Those are the outfits they wear in the music video for 'A Style of Your Own,'" said Rachel. "I love that song!"

"Me, too," Kirsty agreed. "I hope they sing it this afternoon."

Rachel pushed open the café door and the girls went inside.

"Rachel, Kirsty!" called Lexy, one of The Angels, from a table in the big bay window. "Come and join us."

The girls hurried toward Serena, Emilia, and Lexy. But The Angels weren't alone. Sitting with them were five teenagers who were all wearing brown hoodies.

"Kirsty, it's The Groove Gang!" Rachel whispered excitedly as they approached the table. "Looks like we're having brunch with *two* bands instead of one!"

"Fantastic!" Kirsty murmured, her eyes shining. Then she frowned. "But they look so different from the poster. I wonder why they aren't wearing their special colors today. . . ."

Drab Dressers

"Glad you could make it, girls," said Serena with a smile as Kirsty and Rachel sat down. "I'm sure you recognize our friends The Groove Gang?"

"Of course we do!" Kirsty said a little shyly. "Rachel and I *love* your videos. We're always trying to copy your dance moves!"

"Our favorite is 'A Style of Your
Own,'" Rachel added.

Lila smiled at the girls. "Thank you,"
she said. "We love meeting our fans."

"It's a little embarrassing, though,"
Blake said, making a face, "because we
don't have much style today at all!" He
glanced down at his brown hoodie.

"We had an accident
with the washing
machine this
morning,"
explained
Paige. "Our
stylist, Suzy
Sparkle,
washed our
hoodies and the
bright colors got

mixed up in the wash. They all came out brown!"

"Oh, that's too bad," Kirsty said.

"Actually, *all* our clothes turned brown in the wash," Yvette said with a sigh.

"Except our outfits for the concert this afternoon," Rick reminded her. "Don't forget we're picking them up from Suzy after breakfast."

"That's lucky," remarked Emilia. "The Groove Gang just wouldn't be the same

if you didn't all have your special colors to wear." Kirsty looked at the members of The Groove Gang. "Would you mind if Rachel and I took a photo of you?" she asked politely.

"Not at all," Paige replied with a smile. "But maybe you'd rather wait until later, when we've changed into our concert outfits?"

"Yes, we'll look more like ourselves then!" Lila agreed. "We'll be wearing our special, signature colors."

"OK," Kirsty agreed.

Lexy turned to Rachel and Kirsty. "Sorry, girls, but Serena, Emilia, and I aren't looking too great this morning, either!" she said, pointing at her jeans. Rachel and Kirsty saw that they were damp and had muddy stains all over them. Serena's and Emilia's jeans were stained, too, and there was a big splash of mud on Emilia's white T-shirt.

"What happened?" asked Rachel, taking off her raincoat.

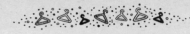

"Did you notice that group of boys jumping around in the puddles near Star Village?" Serena asked. The girls nodded.

"Well, they splashed us with muddy water." Lexy sighed.

Rachel and Kirsty exchanged an anxious look. They knew exactly why the stars were having such bad luck with their outfits. It was because Miley's magic clef was missing! Rachel could feel Miley moving around restlessly inside her shirt pocket, and she guessed that the little fairy was upset by what she was hearing.

"Well, Rachel and I had no dry clothes this morning because the rain leaked into our tent," Kirsty explained, hanging her raincoat on the back of her chair. "That's why we're both wearing things that clash!"

Serena smiled. "Let's forget all about our clothes and enjoy a nice brunch together," she suggested as two waitresses came toward them. The waitresses were carrying trays stacked with plates of pancakes, a pitcher of orange juice, and containers of maple syrup, honey, and jam, which they placed on the table.

"This looks great!" Blake said eagerly.
He reached for a pancake and then
for the maple syrup, but he ended
up dripping sticky
syrup all over
his sleeve.
Serena
handed him
a paper
napkin to
clean it up,
but accidentally
knocked over Paige's glass of orange
juice. The juice ran across the tablecloth
and dripped into Lexy's lap.

Kirsty bit her lip and stole a glance at
Rachel as Yvette dropped a blob of
strawberry jam on her knee. The girls
knew that things would only get worse

for the superstars unless they found
Miley's magic clef. Kirsty wondered
where it could be.

"I think we need another rehearsal
before the concert this afternoon, guys,"
Rick remarked when breakfast was
almost over. "Are you all up for it?"

Blake, Paige, and Lila nodded.

"Aren't we supposed to be picking up
our stage outfits from Suzy now?" asked
Yvette.

"We could get them for you," Kirsty
offered.

"Oh, would you?" Yvette said.
"Thanks, girls! It would give us more
time to rehearse. Could you get them
from Suzy's trailer and bring them over
to the dressing rooms behind the main
stage, please?"

"No problem," said Rachel.

Kirsty, Rachel, The Angels, and The Groove Gang walked back to the festival site together. It was still raining, but not quite as heavily.

"Suzy Sparkle's trailer is that pink, sparkly one over there," Rick told the girls. "Thanks again."

"Thanks for brunch!" Rachel and Kirsty called as The Groove Gang went off to their rehearsal tent and The Angels headed for their trailer. Once they were alone, Miley popped her head out of Rachel's pocket.

"Isn't it a shame about their fabulous clothes?" Miley sighed. "We've got to make sure that *nothing* ruins The Groove Gang's outfits for the concert this afternoon — and that means finding my clef. I can feel that it's here somewhere, close by."

"There must be goblins around here, too," Rachel said as they went over to the bright pink trailer.

"We haven't seen any so far today," Kirsty said.

Miley ducked out of sight again as Kirsty knocked on the glossy pink door.

A young woman with long blond hair, wearing a black lace dress, opened the door. "The Groove Gang asked us to pick up their outfits for this afternoon and take them to their dressing rooms," Kirsty explained.

"They decided to rehearse before the concert," Rachel added.

"Oh, come in!" Suzy Sparkle smiled at them. "You're Rachel and Kirsty, aren't you? I've heard all about you from The Angels." She ushered the girls into the trailer, which had clothes piled everywhere. "Look, these are The Groove Gang's outfits," Suzy went on, pointing at a rack with three short black skirts and two pairs of black pants

hanging on it. Next to them were five colorful shirts. "What do you think, girls?"

"They're fantastic!" Rachel exclaimed. Metallic threads were woven into the shirt material, so they glittered in the light.

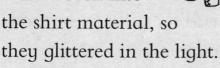

"*And* they're all the right colors," Kirsty said happily, touching the sleeve of Paige's pink shirt. Relieved, she glanced at Rachel. There was nothing wrong with *these* outfits.

Carefully, Suzy began removing the clothes from the rack, and Rachel and Kirsty draped them neatly over their arms.

"Thanks, girls," Suzy said. "At least it stopped raining! See you at the concert."

Rachel and Kirsty left the trailer with the outfits. As they headed toward the dressing rooms, Miley peeked out again.

"The shirts are fabulous, girls!" she declared with a big smile. "We *have to* keep them safe —"

"HEY!"

A loud voice nearby made Rachel and Kirsty jump. Then they saw one of the boys they'd noticed earlier come running toward them. His rain hat was pulled down and his bright green raincoat was flapping around him.

"Look at those shirts!" the boy yelled. "They're amazing!"

Suddenly, the other boys appeared and rushed toward Rachel and Kirsty. The

girls were too surprised to move, and the
boys gathered around them, jumping
in the muddy puddles and trying to grab
the outfits. To Rachel's and Kirsty's
horror, they were both
knocked backward.
They fell into an
enormous, dirty
puddle that
splashed them
and the
clothes they
were carrying.

"Oh, no!"
Rachel gasped,
staring down at the wet and stained
shirts, skirts, and pants. "What is The
Groove Gang going to wear for their
concert *now*?"

Gorgeous Goblin!

"Look what you did!" Kirsty cried, staring angrily at the boys. "You ruined all the outfits!"

Laughing, the boys spun around and ran off, jumping in more puddles as they went. However, one of them was left behind because his boot was stuck in a big patch of sticky mud. Muttering to himself,

he tried to yank his
boot free. Instead,
his enormous foot
jerked out and
left the rain boot
behind. Kirsty and
Rachel could hardly
believe their eyes
when they saw that
his skin was *green*.

"He's a goblin!" Kirsty whispered to
Rachel.

"*All* those boys must be goblins, and
we didn't even realize!" Rachel replied.
"But which one of them has Miley's
magic clef?"

"Rachel, look at his boot," Kirsty
murmured as the goblin finally rescued
his boot and jammed it back onto his

foot. "It's clean and shiny, even though it was stuck in the mud."

"His raincoat's really clean, too, even though he's been splashing around in puddles like the others," Rachel pointed out. "Maybe he has the clef, and it's keeping his clothes from getting dirty."

"I think he does, girls!" Miley exclaimed. "Don't let him get away!"

The goblin raced off now, looking for the others. He ran toward Star Village and then disappeared into the dress-up tent. Rachel and Kirsty were close

behind him, but when they reached the entrance to the tent, they stopped.

"There are lots of people inside," Rachel whispered to Miley. "We don't want anyone to guess what we're up to."

"I'll turn you into fairies, then," Miley whispered back. "But hurry, girls!"

Rachel and Kirsty dove behind a nearby trailer. There, Miley zoomed out of Rachel's pocket and showered the girls with glittery magic that shrank them down to Miley's size and gave them fairy wings. Silently, the three friends fluttered into

the dress-up tent, keeping high above the crowd. They could see the goblin ahead of them, weaving his way between the racks packed with clothes toward the fitting rooms at the other end of the tent.

"Where'd he go?" Miley asked a few minutes later. "Oh, no, I think we lost him, girls."

Rachel and Kirsty looked around anxiously.

"I can see him!" Kirsty announced suddenly. "Well, I can see his feet, at least! Look, there are his big green boots poking out from under that fitting-room door."

"The goblin must have cut in front of everyone in line," Rachel remarked as they flew over a long line of people who were clutching outfits and waiting for the fitting rooms. "I wonder what outfit he took in there."

A moment later, the fitting-room door flew open. Miley, Rachel, and Kirsty hovered above, watching as the goblin strutted out. He was wearing a glittering green jacket and pants, white gloves, dark sunglasses, and a black wide-brimmed hat pulled down

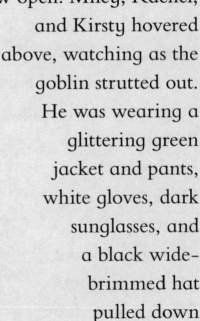

over his face. He looked extremely
stylish, and everyone in the line seemed
to be admiring him.

"That guy looks fantastic!" Rachel
heard a teenage boy say to his friend.
The boy was wearing a blue tracksuit
that was too big for him and a baseball
hat that was too small. "He has to be

the best-dressed
person here."
His friend,
who was
wearing a
bright yellow
tracksuit,
purple
sneakers, and
a bowler
hat, nodded.

"Everyone else's outfits look silly
compared to his, don't they?" he replied.
"Including ours!"

As Rachel stared
at the goblin,
her heart
began to
hammer
with
excitement.
She could
see the magic
clef hanging on
a chain around
his neck!

Silently, Rachel motioned to Miley and
Kirsty. Together, the three of them flew
down and landed on a shelf stacked high
with colorful silk and chiffon scarves.

Meanwhile, the goblin was parading
up and down, pretending that he was
modeling on a catwalk. Everyone
watching applauded enthusiastically.

"The goblin's wearing the clef!"
Rachel murmured to Miley and Kirsty.
"But how are we going to get it back
with all these people around?"

Photo Opportunity

Rachel, Miley, and Kirsty thought about it for a moment.

"I *think* I have an idea," Kirsty said slowly. "Listen, here's what we should do . . ." And quickly she explained her plan.

After taking several bows, the goblin had now headed back into the fitting

room again, leaving the crowd to wait impatiently to see his next outfit.

Quietly, Rachel and Kirsty flew down and landed on the floor behind a rack

packed with clothes. Still perched on the shelf above them, Miley waved her wand and a cloud of magical sparkles floated down around the girls. Within seconds, they were back to their normal size.

Suddenly, the crowd cheered. Rachel and Kirsty ducked out from behind the clothes rack and saw that the goblin had come out of the fitting room and was strutting around again. This time, he was wearing a glittery blue shirt, black

dress pants, gold bracelets, and the same
black hat.

"Ready, Rachel?" Kirsty whispered,
taking her camera out of her pocket.
Rachel nodded and did the same. Then
the two girls stepped out in front of the
goblin.

"Hi, we're taking
pictures for a new
magazine called
Star Style," Kirsty
said quickly.
"We'd love to take
some shots of you."

"Your outfit's
great," Rachel
added. "You're so
stylish. You *have* to
be in our magazine!"

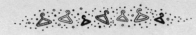

The goblin adjusted his hat. "Yes, I *am* stylish, aren't I?" he said smugly. He put his hands on his hips and posed, and Kirsty and Rachel began snapping away. The crowd watched with interest.

"That's stunning," Kirsty said. "You should be a model!"

The goblin looked very pleased with himself.

"Can we try something a little different?" Rachel asked.

She took a red sequined scarf from the shelf where Miley was still hiding. "I think this would look great in the photos. Could you switch it with that necklace you're wearing now?"

The goblin frowned and touched the magic clef hanging around his neck. Rachel and Kirsty waited patiently, trying not to give their plan away.

Then, to the girls' dismay, the goblin simply tied the scarf around his neck, over the necklace. Kirsty and Rachel exchanged worried glances. The plan hadn't worked! Now they'd have to come up with something else.

"OK, let's see lots of different poses," Kirsty called, trying to keep the goblin interested long enough to give them time to think. "Look this way and smile. Now wave at the camera. Stand on one leg . . ."

The goblin was happy to do everything Kirsty asked. He loved being the center of attention! But Kirsty was beginning to panic because she couldn't think of another way to get the clef back.

"I have an idea!" Rachel whispered. She murmured a few words to Kirsty, who nodded, and then glanced up at the shelf. Miley was peeking out from behind a pile of scarves, and Rachel winked at her.

"I want a really
good shot for
the cover of the
magazine,"
Kirsty called
to the goblin.
"Can you do a
handstand?"

"Of course I
can!" the goblin
declared. He
threw himself onto
his hands and
balanced upside down,
waving his legs in the air. Kirsty
watched with wide eyes as the sequined
scarf slipped over his head and onto the
floor. Then the necklace did exactly
the same thing!

The Groove Gang Rocks!

Rachel glanced up at Miley, who instantly flew off the shelf, hidden underneath a thin lavender-colored scarf. The scarf floated down and landed on top of the necklace. Kirsty breathed a sigh of relief and rushed forward. She quickly scooped up the scarf, along with Miley and the magic clef, which was now back to its

Fairyland size. Then she dropped the
fairy safely into her raincoat pocket.

The goblin gave a
shriek as he lost his
balance and fell
sideways. Rachel
and Kirsty saw the
glitter fade from his
clothes, and the outfit
that had previously
looked so stylish now looked
ridiculous and very sloppy.

"I don't know why we all thought that
guy was so stylish," Rachel heard the
teenage boy murmur to his friend.
"That's the worst outfit I've ever seen!"

The rest of the crowd lost interest in the
goblin, too, as they began to discover all
the gorgeous outfits now hanging on the

racks. Rachel and Kirsty went over to
help him to his feet.

"No one likes
my outfit
anymore,"
the goblin
grumbled.
"Oh, well,
you know how
fashions come
and go," Kirsty
said to him.
"But *your* style
will last forever!"
Rachel told him. "Remember, you just
have to be true to yourself. Don't follow
the crowd!"

The goblin nodded and hurried away.

"That's a quote from The Groove

Gang's song 'A Style of Your Own'!"
Kirsty laughed.

"Speaking of The Groove Gang . . ."
Rachel pulled a sparkly yellow hoodie
and a pair of denim
shorts off a nearby
rack. "Wouldn't
this be perfect for
Yvette to replace
the outfit that
got all muddy?"

"Great idea!"
Kirsty said. "And
I can see something
that would look good on
Blake, too." She showed Rachel a pair of
baggy jeans and a shimmering blue shirt.

"Keep looking, girls," Miley whispered
from Kirsty's pocket. "The magic from

my clef means that there are lots of wonderful superstar clothes to find!"

The girls hunted around the clothing racks, and they soon found stage outfits in all The Groove Gang members' special colors. They even found a couple of very glamorous dresses for themselves, one silver and one gold. Then they hurried out of the tent with their arms full of gorgeous clothes. Now the rain had stopped and the sun was shining down brightly.

Just before the concert began, Rachel and Kirsty, wearing their silver and gold dresses, went back to the dressing rooms. The Groove Gang had asked them to help Suzy Sparkle with any last-minute adjustments to their outfits. When the girls arrived, they were thrilled to see

that the band members were all wearing
the clothes they'd chosen for them.

"These replacement
outfits are great, girls,"
said Lila. She did a
twirl in her short lilac
skirt. "It was not at
all nice of those boys
to splash you with
muddy water like that."

"But we actually like
these new clothes even better!" Rick
exclaimed, showing off the red T-shirt
and red and black pants he was wearing.

Smiling happily, Rachel and Kirsty
helped Suzy Sparkle with the girls' hair
and makeup. They'd just finished fixing
Paige's hair when Blake suddenly
exclaimed, "Hey, you girls wanted a

photo, didn't you? Give your cameras to
Suzy, and she'll take a few shots."

Kirsty and Rachel handed over their
cameras, and Suzy took some photos of
them posing with The
Groove Gang.

"Thank
you!" Rachel
and Kirsty
said, hardly
able to believe
their luck.

"Well, we're
on!" Yvette said,
ushering the others out of the dressing
room. "Enjoy the show, girls."

Rachel and Kirsty hurried out into
the field to watch the concert. As The
Groove Gang ran onstage to wild cheers

and loud applause, Miley fluttered out of Kirsty's little gold handbag.

"You look very glamorous, girls!" Miley said with a smile.

"It's nice to dress like a superstar sometimes," Rachel said with a grin, smoothing down her shiny silver dress. "But I think these clothes are for special occasions only!"

"Hello, Rainspell Island Music Festival!" Blake shouted. "We're really glad to be here, and we just have one thing to say to you — be true to yourself and don't follow the crowd, be stylish and proud!"

The crowd roared its appreciation as The Groove Gang launched into their big hit "A Style of Your Own." Rachel and Kirsty sang along, dancing around while Miley hovered near them.

"I have just enough magic to make sure The Groove Gang's concert is a success," Miley remarked happily. "Thank you for helping me find my clef today, girls."

"We still have three clefs to find," Rachel said. "And we're not going to give up until we have them back, are we, Kirsty?"

Kirsty shook her head as she clapped along to the music. "We *can't* let Jack Frost spoil the rest of the Rainspell Island Music Festival!" she said firmly. "We'll be on the lookout for another clef tomorrow!"

Miley has her magic clef back.
Now Kirsty and Rachel need to help

Frankie
the Makeup Fairy!

Read on for a special sneak peek. . . .

Makeup Mix-up

The sun was shining on best friends
Rachel Walker and Kirsty Tate. It was
summer vacation, and they had come to
the Rainspell Island Music Festival as
special guests of their favorite music
group, The Angels.

The girls were standing in the middle
of a cluster of activity tents known as

Star Village. There were tents of every shape and color, with fortune-tellers, singing teachers, musicians, and stylists offering their services for free. It was hard to know which one to choose!

"Let's try that one," said Rachel.

She pointed to a tent that sparkled in the morning sun. The sign hanging outside said GLITTER & GO, and people were lining up to have their faces painted.

As the girls joined the line, a group of teenagers walked past, chatting about the famous people they had seen.

"I heard that Dakota May's here," said one of the boys.

Kirsty and Rachel gasped. Dakota May was one of their favorite superstars.

"I hope she's going to put on a concert while she's here!" said Kirsty.

They started singing Dakota May's latest song, "The Faces of Me," and they only stopped when it was their turn to have their faces painted. Giggling, the girls hurried into the tent and perched on high stools.

"Hi, I'm Chloe," said a bubbly dark-haired girl to Rachel. "What would you like today?"

Rachel knew exactly what she wanted!

"Could I have a rainbow across my cheek?" she asked.

"Sure thing," said Chloe, picking up her jar of makeup brushes.

"How about you?" asked the red-headed makeup artist in front of Kirsty. "I'm Dora, by the way."

"I can't decide!" said Kirsty with a smile. . . .

RAINBOW magic

These activities are magical!
Play dress-up, send friendship notes, and much more!

RAINBOW magic™

There's Magic in Every Series!

The Rainbow Fairies
The Weather Fairies
The Jewel Fairies
The Pet Fairies
The Fun Day Fairies
The Petal Fairies
The Dance Fairies
The Music Fairies
The Sports Fairies
The Party Fairies
The Ocean Fairies
The Night Fairies
The Magical Animal Fairies
The Princess Fairies
The Superstar Fairies

Read them all!

■ SCHOLASTIC

scholastic.com
rainbowmagiconline.com

HiT entertainment

RMFAIRY7

SPECIAL EDITION

Three Books in Each One— More Rainbow Magic Fun!

Joy the Summer Vacation Fairy
Holly the Christmas Fairy
Kylie the Carnival Fairy
Stella the Star Fairy
Shannon the Ocean Fairy
Trixie the Halloween Fairy
Gabriella the Snow Kingdom Fairy
Juliet the Valentine Fairy
Mia the Bridesmaid Fairy
Flora the Dress-Up Fairy
Paige the Christmas Play Fairy
Emma the Easter Fairy
Cara the Camp Fairy
Destiny the Rock Star Fairy
Belle the Birthday Fairy
Olympia the Games Fairy
Selena the Sleepover Fairy
Cheryl the Christmas Tree Fairy
Florence the Friendship Fairy
Lindsay the Luck Fairy

■SCHOLASTIC

scholastic.com
rainbowmagiconline.com

HIT entertainment

RMSPECIAL10